D0474265

Jimmy's class was taking a field trip to the museum and George was going along.

"We're glad to have you, George," said Mr Chauncy,
the teacher, "but don't get into trouble."

At the museum, Mr Chauncy began to explain one of the displays. "These rocks are millions of years old…" The students weren't listening.

"This is boring," said a student.

"It really is," said another.

"When is lunch time?" asked a third.

George wandered off. He didn't find the rocks very interesting, either.

But in the next room, George saw something very interesting.

It was a huge skeleton. What a long tail!

It was too much for George to resist.

He stepped over the rope and jumped onto the tail.

He climbed down …

... then climbed up.

He climbed up and up until he reached the skeleton's head!

Just then, Mr Chauncy and the class came into the room.

"Look at that dinosaur," said Jimmy.

"And look at George!" he shouted.

"Ride 'im, George," cried a girl.

The guards heard the noise.

"Get down from there," ordered one of them.

"I'm going to get the director," said the other.

George was scared.

"Is that how they rode dinosaurs in the old days?" a girl asked Mr Chauncy.

"Well, no…" he said.

"Tell us more about the dinosaurs," someone said.

George was curious. What was a dinosaur?

"Well," said Mr Chauncy, "the earth was once full of huge creatures like this."

Suddenly, the director of the museum came charging in.

"What's this about a monkey on our dinosaur?" he asked.

"Guards! Get that monkey down before he causes any damage," he ordered.

Poor George. There he was on top of a dinosaur …

with no place to hide!

"Just a moment," said Mr Chauncy. "George was a great help to me. He got the children interested in the dinosaurs."

"We wouldn't have listened," said a boy.

"It's so interesting," said another.

"I want to come back again," said a girl.

"Well," said the director, "I can see that our dinosaur isn't damaged. We'll forgive him this time."

"You can come down, George," he called.

"Hooray!" the students shouted.

Mr Chauncy said, "I have to thank you for making this visit an interesting one, George. But next time, promise not to ride the dinosaur."

When the bus stopped in front of George's house, the man in the yellow hat was waiting. "I'm glad to see you, George," he said. "I hope you kept out of trouble today."